To Hen
May you travels
be adventurous!

SALEM SWITCH

BY

~~JESSICA LUCCI~~

Jessica Lucci

Copyright

Salem Switch

by Jessica Lucci

Dedication

Dedicated to the people who lost their lives during the Salem Witch Trials.

About this Book

Professor Tess Alset is transported back in time 200 years to 1690 in Salem, Massachusetts, where magic and evil lurk. She and her clones are accused of witchcraft and must devise a way to flee back to their own time before they are murdered in the Salem Witch Trials. Things get more complicated when a beautiful woman befriends the small group of allies, but she is much more than she appears to be. The nearby tribe of Native Americans offer their help just as the powerful reverend leads the charge in spiritual, physical, and paranormal battle. What risks will Tess take in order to achieve fame, love, and prominence? Is her life worth the glory attached to death? Only time will tell.

Book reviews are the best way to communicate your literary opinions with an author and other readers. Please review "Salem Switch" on Amazon and Goodreads!

CHAPTER 1

A flash of lightening burst inside the cold laboratory and a sonic boom shook the foundation. The lanterns flickered as a loud squawk echoed in the concrete chamber.

"Dag nabbit, the bird is still here! Come, Lamarr. I'm glad to see you, but I had hoped to send you on a time travel adventure." The blue budgerigar hopped on little clawed feet and flew lightly to Tess's outstretched finger. Tess cooed at the quaint creature. "You have done a fine job. The failure is mine, not yours." She set Lamarr down onto an elaborate perch, a veritable bird playground with spinning mirrors, ramps and ladders, swings and slides. Lamarr chewed some hanging millet, her reward for work well done.

"That's the third time we've tried that," lamented Tess. "What in the heck are we doing wrong?" She flopped into her high backed seat at the lab table and ground her fists into her eyes.

Verdandi untwined a wrench from Tess's knotted black hair. "I know you are using work to distract yourself from your breakup with Hugh, but you are allowed to feel your sadness." Tess grunted an unladylike reply.

Verdandi pressed a remote control knob on her prosthetic arm, and a tea tray floated over. She poured chamomile tea to settle Tess's nerves. Tess felt relief enter her body with the first sip of soothing liquid. She was finally coaxed into taking a break when Verdandi implored her with additional trays of scones.

Tess spread cream and jam over her hot pastry. "Thank you for tempting me to rest, dear child. I am overwrought with frustration. Failure after failure is diminishing my zest." She took a dainty bite of her sweet treat.

"It is okay to take a breather. You are allowed."

Tess placed the scone down onto her delicate China plate. Fiery fervor flashed in her blue eyes. "I need to be the one to discover time travel and invent conductors between eras. I must be first."

"Why, is it a contest? Can't you enjoy the process just as well without the sense of competition?"

"I must be the one," Tess insisted. She replaced her plate onto the hovering tray. "More than anything in the world, I wish to be the one who discovers time travel. Imagine the possibilities!"

"I can imagine, Professor," answered Verdandi. She had been an apprentice to the great mastermind for a number of years and now that she was a young woman, she felt a kinship with her, as well as awe at her mentor's genius. "Yet part of what I imagine is etched with fear. You lack patience with yourself. If you could extend the patience you offer me to yourself, you might be able to release anxiety and see your work from a different perspective."

The professor smiled and held her hand over the student's warm flesh one. "I am lucky to have such a darling, intelligent girl look out for me. I appreciate your assistance. I know my pride is mighty, but that is part of what drives me to create world changing inventions."

Verdandi's freckled face flushed with the kind words her idol nourished her with. "I am glad to learn from you. Now I am old enough to understand more than you might realize. I do not mean solely in the maths and sciences. I mean in matters of the heart."

Tess removed her hand from Verdandi's and raised an eyebrow.

"I understand that your heart is broken over the severed relationship you have recently experienced with Hugh. It seems that you are frantically working in an effort to distract yourself from your feelings."

Tess sighed and brushed invisible crumbs from her long skirts.

"I still believe that what has been ripped can be patched up," Verdandi added carefully.

Tess jumped up from her seat, upsetting Lamarr who had hopped over to nibble on a broken scone while the two scientists talked.

"What is it?" asked Verdandi. She was not alarmed at this sudden change of attitude; rather she was curious. When inspiration struck the professor, it struck hard.

Lamarr flew to the crown of Tess's head. "We have attempted to send you back 200 years three times already," said Tess gently. "I think that is enough."

"We could try again," said Verdandi.

Tess's eyes shone. "We will." Lamarr flew back to her birdie playground.

"I love this bird... I love this bird as a man loves a woman. But better." Her face clouded over with the memory of Hugh's sharp words. "This time, we will try again, but we will try it differently. It's time to up our game, raise the stakes, for sciences sakes."

Tess stood beneath the glass dome attached to the knife switch on the far wall.

Verdandi pulled the switch. Again and again. Three times, lightening struck; three times the earth rumbled. And three times, the genius professor fumed with the flame of failure. She left the dome and lay herself down next to the bird's colourful hut. Lamarr hopped atop her forehead. "Thank you for caring, Lamarr."

A rustle of feathers gusted over them. A white pigeon settled on the large perch by the window and lifted a leg. Verdandi retrieved the message.

"The mail service has delivered an odd looking scroll, addressed to you," said Verdandi.

"Read it please," said Tess, covering her eyes with her forearm as she lay back.

"Dear Professor Alset,

The answer to your conundrum lies in the transformer's conveyor. Convert the variations of current into an arc, joined by a hoop at both ends. This will disperse the units of energy at regular recurring intervals, necessary for your mission.

P.S. Please bring scones."

"It is unsigned?" Tess asked wearily from her resting place.

"Yes, but I think there is merit to it."

"I am succumbing to sleep. I'll attempt to dream up a resolution."

"As will I," said Verdandi, studying the note and making computations in her head.

While the professor napped, the student tackled the time travel contraption. She adjusted the arc calibrations and changed the power grid to the switch.

Tess awoke amidst a harsh autumn rain storm. The glass roof showed only grey clouds and misty raindrops, and the whoosh of wind echoed in the hollow chamber.

Lightening burst from the clouds. Tess stood on top of a pedestal beneath the glass dome. "Flip the switch!"

"No, it's too dangerous under these conditions."

"I'm the professor! I know what I'm doing. This is my invention, after all. Flip the switch!"

With two hands, Verdandi lifted the heavy handle. Sparks flew as the arc lamp lighted and shone with dazzling light of fireworks. Yellow, then red, then blue, then green. Verdandi closed her eyes to the scorching brightness. Her face was flecked with flying shards of burning metal. The laboratory shook while the wind outside roared as if alive with anger. Inside the lab, papers flew from an invisible source, and a loud pop burst the ceiling. Shards of glass rained down.

"Professor!" shouted Verdandi.

Lamarr squawked.

Where the professor had stood was only a swirl of green smoke.

Professor Tess Alset was gone.

Verdandi knelt to the wet floor as the generator yet sparked. Wires hung limply from the cords of currentless connections.

"She did it," whispered the young scientist. "She has travelled back two hundred years, if her calibrations were correct, to 1693. Or she is dead." She held her head in her hands as her wet red hair stuck to her face, and cried.

CHAPTER 2

Tess fell to wet ground covered in red leaves. For a moment she thought she was dead. The earth rumbled beneath her like a hungry monster ready to swallow her up. She raised herself unsteadily to her feet and assessed her surroundings.

All around her were tall black trees with naked branches reaching through a silver sky. Her laboratory was gone. Or rather she was gone. Had she done it? Had she travelled back two hundred years?

She spun slowly around in a pebbly puddle, not caring that her face was plastered by her wet jet black hair or that her dripping skirts clung to her trembling legs. Then she halted her circle of reconnaissance. Her mouth opened in an astonished oval.

Three figures emerged from the pine woods. Three shapes of the same size and build. Three faces identical to her own.

The three women rushed toward her, and Tess was too stunned to move. One of them threw a colourful woven blanket over Tess's face and body. This jolted her back into action.

"Unhand me! Let me go!" She struggled against the three women who said nothing, but continued wrapping her in the blanket so tightly that she could not escape. Only her feet revealed themselves, kicking in short bursts, hitting nothing. The trio hoisted the squirming bundle to their shoulders and carried her to a small lean-to within a shallow cave.

"We are going to release you now," said a familiar voice. "You will be surprised, but if you trust us, we can explain."

Tess made a grunt of a promise and she was unwound from her prison. She was unceremoniously rolled out onto sandy ground. She let her eyes adjust to the darkness of the cave. What she saw stunned her, so she could not breathe.

Before her, were three clones, matching her right down to every lush eyelash. Even their clothes were the same.

"Hello, Tess," spoke one. "We understand that you might be afraid,"

"Or shocked," said another,

"Or awed," said the third.

"But let me assure you of your sanity," continued the first. "We are three Tesses. We have decided to call ourselves T1, T2, and T3, for simplicity's sake."

Tess shook her head, dazed by what she saw. She was silent as her brain shot with electric decisions and reconstructions. She met T1's eyes. "But I am T1. I am the first one. I am the only one."

T3 answered her. "We are you, and you are us. We could call you "Tess" instead of "T4" since you are the original, I suppose." T1 and T2 nodded in agreement.

"We could make you some tea, if we had any," said T2.

T1 peered close to Tess's face eagerly. "Did you bring any scones?"

Tess took three deep breaths. She was sane. She was real. She was uninjured. So this must be truth without illusion. "Could you," she said slowly, "help me understand our situation?"

"Of course," said T3. "But first you must remove those wet clothes before you catch a cold. T1 and T2, please restart the fire. Even without the comfort of tea, we can cozy up and explain to the best of our abilities. Then we can make a plan on how to proceed."

After Tess was adequately warmed up within a cocoon of the rainbow coloured blanket, soaking up the heat of the fire, the clones began their explanation.

"We knew you had arrived," began T3, "because of the earthquake."

"You mean the earth rumbling was not a phenomenon exclusively experienced by me?"

"Correct," added T1. "The earthquake reached as far as the town of Salem, wherein we lie on the outskirts."

T2 continued the tale. "We are in hiding because each time one of us appeared, the townsfolk cried out, screaming about witchcraft and howling about their crumbled church steeple and fallen chimneys."

"We all found each other and hid in this cavern," concluded T3, "where we were further surprised, and saved, by the Natives. They showed us how to make a lean-to and gave us this blanket, and fish to cook."

"Fish? And you ate it?" All three clones nodded. "But I am, I mean we are, we do not eat meat!"

"True," said T3 sadly, "yet when it comes to following our habits or facing starvation, I choose to eat."

"I suppose you are right," said Tess. "But look," she pulled a linen handkerchief from deep in her pockets. "I brought scones!"

"Huzzah!" cried the clones. T3 hugged Tess. "You're the best."

Tess beamed. "I suppose I am."

After eating, the group of would-be sisters cuddled up to nap by the dwindling fire. The sky was black now, but no stars shone through the murky depths of midnight.

Beyond their dreams, a raven cawed.

They were awakened by a rectangle of orange sun edging its way into the lean-to. Then they heard a voice.

"Hello, anyone at home?"

"You three hide behind the blanket," Tess whispered. "I will go investigate."

Tess stepped out of the darkness into a bright autumn day. The cloudless sky was pure blue, and still shone with a half moon.

"Good morning, good woman," said the voice.

Tess observed the person before her. She was a tall comely woman, with blonde

20

hair softly curling beneath the hood of her black cloak. In her hands was a large wicker basket.

"I saw your fire in the night and worried that there may be a person of need nearby. And so I have brought you these apples, to nourish you and give you strength. Here, take one." The woman removed an orange scarf from her face, revealing her beauty. She plucked an apple from the basket and handed it to Tess.

"Thank you." Tess curtsied.

"I am Goodwoman Hazel Feathergill. You may simply call me Hazel. And you are?"

"I am Prof- you can simply address me as Tess."

"Yes, Tess, what a lovely name."

"Thank you," blushed the professor.

"You are welcome. Is there anything I can do to assist you?"

"No, I am fine, I was just going to take my morning tea, but it seems as if it is scarce. Yet I'll get by without it."

Hazel smiled warmly. "I know how to brew a delightful tea. Why don't I empty this basket of apples here by your abode and we can go foraging together?"

"That would be lovely." Tess hurridly emptied the apples next to the lean-to, not wanting Hazel to sneak a glimpse inside. She didn't know how much she could trust this beautiful stranger.

"Be sure to wear your scarf."

Tess was flustered. "I must admit I do not have one."

"No matter; you can use a freshly laundered one of mine." She handed a silky scarlet scarf to Tess. Tess wrapped it around her neck.

"No silly. Around your mouth. You must wear it as law. It is to not catch witchcraft. Everyone must wear one. We wouldn't want you to be arrested on your first day here."

How did she know it was my first day here, wondered Tess. Then she realized that it must be obvious by her meager supplies and poor way of living.

Hazel eyed her up and down. "You aren't from around here, are you?"

"No, I was just visiting, and I became," Tess paused and sniffed the salty air. "Shipwrecked?"

"You poor dear thing. Come with me, I will conjure just the salve to liven you up."

"I am grateful, and will accompany you on this walk." Tess projected her voice so that the clones would be able to hear her behind the blanket within the lean-to.

"Indeed," said Hazel.

On the way to the woods they passed by a flock of three blue budgies. "That is strange, I have never seen that kind of bird before," remarked Hazel. "What a glorious shade of blue, not unlike your eyes."

Tess damned herself for blushing again but gazed in wonderment at the three replicas of Lamarr.

Beyond them, a black shadow hovered.

Upon the professor's return, and Hazel's leaving, the four Tesses discussed important matters over freshly brewed wild berry tea.

"How much can we truly trust Hazel?" asked T1.

"You gave her our real name!" exclaimed T2.

"MY real name," corrected Tess. "I stopped myself before telling her too much. But we are in 1693, after all, not 1893. No one has ever heard of us, or shall I say me, here. Nobody knows I am, we are, a famous inventor."

"No one should find out; it could be disastrous."

"Or helpful," wondered another Tess.

Then the clones showed Tess what they had worked on all morning while she had distracted their visitor.

"We built a stove and a flue from stones so that we can cook food and warm ourselves without inhaling that nasty smoke. And look, we attached pulleys to re-use the steam and power a hot water heater so we can bathe!"

"Wherever did you get the ropes for the pulleys?" asked Tess.

The clones pulled up their skirts, revealing bare legs. "Your stockings!" laughed Tess. "How clever!"

Tess's admiration soon gave way to jealousy.

"I know what you are thinking," said T3, "and we have already discussed it. There is no need for you to abandon us; we can all work together. It will be better that way. And we agree to give you full credit for any discoveries or inventions we might achieve."

Tess breathed a sigh of relief. "That is all well and good, but we need to set our priorities straight. We must recreate the time travel technology so that we can get back to our own time and show off our creation."

"First thing's first," said T3, handing Tess a scrap of birch bark and a burnt twig.

Tess held the two items in her hands and then leaned over onto a rock. She began:

"Dear Professor Alset..."

CHAPTER 3

Hazel reappeared the next morning with an offer to forage for chives deeper in the woods. The misty air held a mid-autumn chill. Tess shivered. Hazel reached out an arm and embraced her beneath the long folds of her cloak. The warmth was instantaneous.

They approached a clearing in the woods. Tess slipped on a patch of wet leaves and Hazel grabbed her arm, saving her from a disastrous fall.

"Thank you," flustered Tess.

"Thank YOU, for accompanying me on my daily walk. It is pleasant to have someone to share my time with."

Clouds suddenly dispersed and a rush of sunlight bore down upon them. Autumn trees shone like a kaleidoscope of fire. The crunch of newly fallen leaves reminded Tess of home, of walking with Hugh along Algonquin trails.

"Whats on your mind? You seem far away."

"Just lost in the past," said Tess.

"I try to focus on the present. For instance, right now I am enjoying the peace of company doing nothing together."

"I am enjoying your company as well." Tess smoothed out her skirts. "Sometimes looking at what I've got reminds me of what I've lost."

"You can be lost with me. I'll show you the way out of the woods any time."

Tess smiled. "Or into the woods!"

"Your smile is beautiful," murmured Hazel.

"That must be my mother's fault." Tess's blue eyes darkened with the pain of living life as an orphan, without a mother she never knew. That sense of loss drew her closer to Verdandi, who was also parentless.

Hazel brushed a stray lock of black hair from Tess's face and tucked it behind her ear.

Then her hand cupped Tess's reddening cheek, and they both leaned in for a whisper of a kiss.

Above them, a chorus of birds chirped. They looked up and saw the three blue budgies perched together, singing happily on a birch branch.

A deep caw broke through the orchestra. Swiftly and silently, a giant raven swooped from a high pointed spruce and grabbed the three pretty birds in its long shining talons.

"Oh no!" Tess fell to her knees. "My sweet Lamarrs."

Hazel held a steady stare at the raven as it zoomed away with its prey.

CHAPTER 4

Reverend Jeremiah Thorndale prepared his sermon for the following Sunday. His people of Salem were in danger. He could feel it. An evil curse was upon them, pushing children into defiance and egging on the egos of women. He pored over his worn leather-bound Bible for the perfect aspect to provide clarity. He found Psalm 137:9.

"Happy shall he be, that taketh and dasheth thy little ones against the stones."

His brown teeth clenched together as he scribbled furiously in his journal, deciphering the Lord's words to the best of his ability for his stubborn church. The face coverings he had ordered him to wear may protect them from inhaling demons, but witchcraft was surely afoot. Better to defeat the smallest threats before they grew into giant beasts.

A large raven flew into his open window and perched on the Bible's pedestal. Around its left leg was bound a message. Reverend Thorndale unwrapped and read it.

"Past the House of the Seven Gables, in the Devil's Den cave, you will find the source of indiscretion upon Salem."

The bird soared off with a screech.

CHAPTER 5

On the third day, Hazel walked into the lean-to with a cheerful greeting. She dropped her bouquet of sunflowers when she saw not just Tess, but three identical copies of her, leaning over a row of cylindrical rocks. She stepped upon the flowers, crushing them beneath her black boots, in her haste to leave.

"Wait!" cried Tess. "I can explain."

Hazel stopped short and Tess almost crashed into her.

"How do you explain that magic, that witchcraft?" Hazel's eyes narrowed as T3 emerged from the lean-to.

"These are my sisters," said Tess. "Please do not go."

The witch peered at T1 and T2 who hid in the shade of the lean-to, listening with keen ears.

"Beyond your sisters," said Hazel, "I am concerned with the items of magical enterprise that you were all hovering over."

"Oh, the pistons? We are simply trying to make...something."

"You mean you are trying to build an addition to your hut?"

"You could say that," said Tess.

Hazel let out a deep breath, took a step closer to Tess, and removed her scarf. Tess could feel the warmth of her breath as she spoke. "You could be accused of witchcraft. What you are doing, hiding in the woods, without a man's company, is suspicious. You could be torched just for that!"

"Please, help me, help us, to not be revealed."

"What promise do I have of yours, if I choose to believe you."

Tess laid her hands gently upon Hazel's caped shoulders. "You have the vow of my friendship."

Overhead a raven creaked on barren branches. Hazel's green eyes gleamed. "I will take your word and keep it close. Your secret is safe with me."

"Thank you," said Tess.

"You are welcome," said Hazel, kissing her cheek.

T3 stepped forward. "What shall we do now?"

Hazel twirled her scarf. "Tess and I will scout the woods for a safer place for you to build a little house. While we do that, you three, sisters, can clear out the lean-to and hide any evidence that you were there.

"I'll just need a moment to grab the blanket for warmth, as we walk," said Tess.

"I will keep you warm," murmured Hazel.

"In that case," said T3, "I am coming too." This romance between Tess and Hazel confounded her, and made her feel a giddy mixture of jealousy and glee.

"No," we will be quite fine just the two of us," said Hazel.

"I insist," said T3. She turned to Tess. "Let us rip the blanket in two so we can each have a shawl as we walk along."

Hazel waited outside of the lean-to. The raven left the branch and slowly spiraled down.

T1 and T2 hastily prepared to leave. They dismantled the lean-to and buried the pistons nearby so they could be retrieved later. The noon sun rose, offering some warmth as the women's breaths came in hot bursts of mist.

"What do you think of Tess and Hazel?" asked T1.

T2 used her hands to sweep around the covered pistons so they would not be found by anyone out of the loop. "I think it is sweet, but does that mean we are all romantic with her now?" The possibilities danced through her mind.

"No, no, that is not how it works," said T1. "Besides, aren't you still too angry with Hugh to even consider a romantic relationship?"

"I suppose I am. He was so rude to me. Thinking he could do a better job than I on the new motor, disparaging my expertise, and siding with Verdandi no less, when it came time to implant the radiator into the new machine. Taking the word of my student over me! It was insulting."

"Then again," said T1, "the girl is brilliant."

"That doesn't mean she was right."

"What if she was?"

T2 bristled. "Even if she was right, Hugh had no cause to be so rude."

"Agreed."

T1 and T2 finished their task and brushed the dust from their skirts.

"What do you say we have a nap," asked T2.

"Quite well."

The two clones huddled together side by side and closed their eyes.

Hazel offered scarves to Tess and T3.

"Thank you," said T3.

"It will keep you safe from witchcraft and colds," said Hazel. "Now if you continue to follow me up this way, I know of a spot that would be good for you to build a little cabin. We had a nasty storm here recently so there are many large branches available to stack and weave together. If we hurry, we can get a start before dark."

"And then bring T1 and T2, I mean our sisters, back with us." said T3.

"Yes, of course," said Hazel. "Your sisters."

T3 pulled her half of the blanket tighter around her shoulders. Hazel wrapped her arm around Tess's waist as they walked. T3 blushed and walked faster ahead of them.

"I'll just scout a bit to see how the terrain is. Call out to me if I need to change direction."

"Will do," said Hazel, pulling Tess even closer so that their thighs brushed against each others beneath their skirts.

Hazel bent her neck down and whispered into Tess's ear. "I admit I wanted to get some time with you alone."

Tess tentatively wrapped her arm around Hazel's waist. Together, they trailed after the clone in warm silence.

T3 scurried along. She wanted no part of whatever romance was kindling between Tess and that stranger. Or did she? She was sure Tess was going soft, and yet it would be nice to have someone to comfort her as Hazel was doing for Tess. So much had happened in so short a time. What if Hazel could be friends with each of them, and offer some camaraderie? She was already proving to be an ally in these cold confusing circumstances. Then again, T1 and T2 had been with her from the beginning. She took a deep breath, held it for the count of three, and let it out slowly. How silly of her to fog her mind with emotion when she drastically needed to concentrate on survival.

She was so lost in her thoughts she almost didn't realize she had reached a hilltop. She stopped to catch her breath and spun around. The sky had cleared and autumn trees surrounded her in a ring of colour. Then she saw it. A little at first, like a snake slithering up into nothingness, then like a bucket of coal dust being unleashed in the wind.

Smoke! Black smoke, coming from the direction of the lean-to! This was no ordinary campfire. This was danger. Had those fool cohorts of hers decided to burn the lean to? That would only attract the wrong attention. She hoped they hadn't been that naive. Then she considered the alternatives, and wished they HAD been that naive.

She slid down the leafy hill and raced back to where Hazel and Tess were slowly catching up.

"Witches!" shouted Reverend Thorndale. "Capture them!"

T1 and T2 sprang to their feet but it was too late. A throng of farmers attacked them, knocking them to the ground and rolling them in the dirt. Thick ropes entwined the two clones' hands and feet together so they could not move. They lay side by side on the cold ground, their hair mussed, their faces muddied, and their dresses torn.

"Look at them, how they wriggle like worms," boomed the reverend's voice. "They are Satan's bait! We will not be caught!"

Women in the crowd gasped. "There are two of them, exactly alike! How eerie, how strange, how unnatural!"

"What shall we do with them now?" asked a burly man with a pitchfork pointed at the trapped clones.

"They need to be brought to court, to God's justice," answered Reverend Thorndale.

Title:	Salem Switch
Cond:	Acceptable
User:	bs_maria
Station:	Wokstationstation1-Malu
Date:	2022-10-10 13:26:54 (UTC)
Account:	Bay State Book Company LLC
Orig Loc.	30-G
mSKU:	BSM.77JI
Seq#.	351
unit_id:	6345997
width:	0.27 in
rank:	2,775,568

delist unit# 6345997

XXXXX

"We have enough court right here," said a young woman. "And I can provide testimony that they are guilty!"

"Testify!" shouted the crowd.

"Two days ago I was forced to leave my duties at the swine barn. I was taken very ill all over and felt a great pricking in the soles of my feet, and after a while I saw apparently the dirty shadows of these two demons, who, as I was sitting in a chair by the fire pulled me down to the ground, and tormented and pinched me very much, and I saw them go away at the door, in which fit I was dumb and so continued till the next morning, finding a great load and heaviness upon my tongue."

"Aye," another young woman spoke. "I too was attacked in such a way. It was just one day ago, when, upon treating the manure in the back gardens that there appeared to me the shape of some two women, who seemed to look and speak most fiercely and angrily, and beat, pinched and afflicted me very sorely telling me not to tend the fields, and I was knocked about senseless and knew not yet I saw who afflicted me. Now I see my attackers, right before my eyes!" The young woman began to cry.

"I also have testimony," called out a weak looking farmer. His clothes were tattered and his breath smelled of booze. "These two wenches cast a spell that immobilized my oxen, making it impossible to harvest my field. I will be ruined for the winter because of this evil!"

"What shall we do with them?" cried out a woman.

Reverend Thorndale opened his Bible. "Ye shall utterly destroy all the places, wherein the nations which ye shall possess served their gods, upon the high mountains, and upon the hills, and under every green tree: And ye shall overthrow their altars, and break their pillars, and burn their groves with fire; and ye shall hew down the graven images of their gods, and destroy the names of them out of that place."

"Burn them, burn them!" chanted the crowd in loud echoes.

The crowd gathered dry leaves and buried T1 and T2 beneath them. The reverend set flint to rock.

The sound of flames filled the air instantly. There was no gentle whoosh nor a cozy crackle. There was only a burning blaze of air being emptied of oxygen. The blankness was filled by flames, so fast and fierce that the reverend had to jump backwards before fire felt his face.

The colours of autumn leaves merged into one hot orange ball. Swirling with all hues of the sun and scalding with a comparable heat, the fire devoured the women.

The screams of the clones brought cheers to the crowd. Their dresses wafting in the wind of fire were the only evidence that they still lay there in the pyre as their voices faded away in black smoke.

The cracking of wood and bones shuffled the flaming grave. The horror of being burned alive was a nasty oily cooking smell, that of fat dripping sausages frying in the pan. The fire sizzled as internal vestibules of slimy liquid hit the ashes. The victim's bodies were transformed to hot beams of light, sparking as the metal on their corsets began to glow white. Their skirts danced in the moving fire, an endless silent song with no musician but death at play.

Blood burst through capillaries, adding spits of liquid to the fire that ceased to slow.

The flame obediently burned away the lives of T1 and T2, not stopping until nothing was left of them, nothing but charred skulls with blistered grins.

Satisfied, the crowd left, without tears.

T3 and Tess and Hazel raced back as quickly as they could. Gone was the prickly chill; now there was just sweat and gasping breath.

T3 took the lead and turned back to see Tess close behind her with Hazel falling behind. "Hurry up!" she cried. Then she struck something so hard, with such force, that she fell onto her back with her feet flailing in the air.

A glorious woman with long braids of black cherry hair reached down to her.

"Am I dead? Are you God?" T3 was slightly concussed and had trouble forming words.

"I am Chief," came the smooth voice from the strong figure. Tess and Hazel caught up breathlessly. "Come, I will show you a quicker way."

Tess looked at her fallen clone and then at Hazel. "I feel as if we have no better choice."

"So be it," grunted Hazel.

"I can't walk, my ankle, it hurts!" wailed T3. "Go on without me."

Chief shook her head and scooped T3 up from the ground and carried her piggy back style the rest of the way.

Tess was first on the scene, followed by Chief and T3. Hazel was the last to arrive.

What they saw made Tess and her clone vomit.

The horror of deranged death lingered with an unholy smell. It was not the crisp smell of burnt leaves that filled Tess's nostrils, but the decay of human organs cooked from the inside out, that churned her guts.

Chief lowered T3 gently to the ground where she knelt and howled in mourning. "We had survived together! How could this happen?"

Hazel crept up behind her.

"I should have been here," sobbed T3.

"Yes, you should have been," Hazel whispered.

Chief circled the pyre. "There must have been more than two dozen of them, women and men combined, and a few children, too," she said, surveying the scene. "It would not have mattered if you had been here or not; their fates were sealed by tyranny."

T3 stood up shakily. "We must rush to town and get vengeance! Or justice! Or something!" Her voice cracked with anger and her face was wet with the depths of mourning.

It was then that Tess saw T3 as if for the first time, not as a nameless clone, but as a separate entity of herself. Tess had not stopped looking at the clones as imposters. When she saw T3 in mourning she realized they were more than extensions of herself; their own persons.

The earth shook. T3 fell to the charred ground. Green lightening pierced the veil of black clouds that had suddenly overtaken the sky. The dwindling smoke from the dead clones dissipated to blue, then was gone.

Tess took off. It couldn't be, she thought to herself. She ran to the place where she had been found just three days prior by her three clones. T3 limped toward her with the help of Chief. Hazel stayed behind, staring into the remnants of T1 and T2.

"Impossible," Tess whispered. Tears filled her eyes.

"Nothing is impossible, dear Professor." Red hair flowed in the smoky wind.

Verdandi had appeared.

CHAPTER 6

"How long has it been? Days seem like weeks. It feels like I haven't seen you in years." Verdandi hugged Tess tightly.

"Suspension and wormhole extraction can effectively loosen dates and times from the current stasis of the calendar," said Tess.

Verdandi giggled. "Dear Professor, I only meant that I missed you." Verdandi looked past Tess and her eyes widened. "There are two of you?"

"I'll explain. Right now we are in a crisis." Tess filled Verdandi in on all she had experienced since time traveling to 1693. "If only we could get back to our own time."

"But we can," smiled Verdandi, revealing a contraption kept safely in the basket she wore across her back. "I wouldn't leave home without it."

"What is it?"

"It is our way, back to the future."

"Where did you get this?" Tess marveled at the intricacies of the creation.

"I made it myself, with the tools and equipment you had prepared at your laboratory table."

"You mean, you discovered a way to travel forward to our own time and invented a device to do so?"

"I suppose I did," said the red head.

"That is incredible."

"One of us had to be less tempestuous and plan ahead. When you didn't return, I guessed what had happened and wanted to chase after you. I had to rig up mechanisms to flip the switch for me, but that was the least of my trouble. I had to decipher a way to bring you back with me. Supposing of course that I didn't sporadically combust."

"You are so brave," said Tess. "Let us leave at once."

"Wait," said T3. "We still have our sisters to avenge."

Tess took T3's hands lightly in hers. "I know how much their deaths have saddened you. My heart, too, breaks for them, and what might have been for all of us together. We will never find out what great things our combined minds could have conquered in the realm of science. Alas, vengeance will not bring them back, and will only place us in more danger. Come back with me, sister, to home, to safety."

Verdandi stepped in. "I understand you are tempted to flee back to our own time. Yet we now bear the responsibility of our progress. We need to remain here until this witch hunt ends. If we cannot help others who are accused, and believe me, there will be, then there will be no end to the murder, and your sisters will have died in vain. We must stay and put an end to this all. It is our duty as ministers of the future to protect the past."

Tess turned to Verdandi and stroked her freckled cheek. "Young one, you are wise beyond your years. Forgive me for my instinct to retreat. I wish to be safe and to ensure the salvation of those closest to me." She looked back and forth at Verdandi and T3. Then her eyes wandered to Hazel, who appeared to be in a heated discussion with Chief. "You are right; we shall stay and see this misery through to the end."

Chief walked towards the little group. "My people would like to offer you our help."

"Thank you," said Tess, "but I think we can manage on our own. We are stronger than we look."

Chief nodded. "I believe you, yet I offer again, set aside your pride and accept the blessing before you. There is no need to suffer more when aid is in your presence. Denying my people's assistance is not just denying yourself, but also denying the safety of your cherished ones and the ones who will experience the future yet to come."

T3 curtsied before the Chief. "I am eternally grateful for your auspicious aid. Please allow me to be of use to you."

The chief's solemn face was betrayed by a twinkle in her eyes. "We do not use people here, but your company would be a welcome pleasure." T3 blushed in delight.

"I apologize," said Tess. "Of course we will accept your help. Strong as we are, we will be stronger together.

Hazel excused herself after being stared down by Chief. She kissed Tess on the cheek with a promise to return.

Chief and her tribe helped Tess, Verdandi, and T3 build a comfortable little shack with two rooms; one with a thatched bed, the other with a strong stable table to work at. It was completed by late evening, just as swirls of rainbow colours spread across the starry sky.

"I have never seen this phenomenon before," said Tess in delight. "I wonder what is causing it.

"It is beautiful, and makes me feel warm," said T3.

Chief smiled at T3. "It is good that you feel the warmth from the sky. What you are witnessing is Nanahbozho, creator of the earth, reminding us with little fires that we are not alone. We are safe."

T3 snuggled into the coyote skin blanket Chief had given her. "Despite all that has happened today, I do feel safe, here, with you."

"I am glad." Chief reached over and held her hand. "I will make it my job to keep you safe, as long as you are with me."

T3 fell into peaceful dreams while Verdandi and Tess stayed up all night whispering by the open campfire. They had plans to make and contraptions to fashion if they wanted to continue their objective of creating peace in Salem before returning home.

In the morning, Tess and Verdandi hovered over the work table and tinkered with found objects. T3 finished cleaning up from the breakfast of quail eggs Chief had shown her how to find. They heard a loud bird call nearby.

"I don't like the sound of that," shuddered Tess.

"Let's go check it out," said Verdandi.

T3 joined them outside where they saw a large Raven perched on a shattered tree stump. It was staring at them with a cocked head, as if it had been waiting for them to emerge.

"I don't like the looks of that bird," said Verdandi.

"I thought you loved all animals," said Tess.

"Not that one. It has a sinister aura about it."

"That's plain silly," said T3. "There are no such thing as sinister auras. It is simply reminding you of the death of the three Lamarrs..."

"And the death of our sisters," said Tess.

The raven cawed and flapped away.

"That is giving me an idea," said Tess. "We could design a flying machine and spy on the townsfolk from above. They will never think to look up. People seldom do."

"Way to take something bad and turn it in to something good," applauded Verdandi.

"Thank you. Now let's get to work."

Verdandi, Tess, and T3 tinkered all the rest of the day on the flying machine. By noon, much of it was complete. T3 excused herself; she had promised to assist Chief with her fishing net, and share technologies.

A shadow lurked at the open doorway. "What have we here?"

Tess jumped from the bed and Verdandi quickly covered the contraption with the coyote skin Chief had left for them.

The figure in the doorway was silhouetted by the sun. Tall and full, with a curved waist that did not rely on a bustier for shape. Tess breathed heavily. "Hazel, my dear, you frightened me. Do come in."

Hazel stepped in, her face yet shadowed. "What have you beneath that savage cadaver?"

Tess's face reddened with a sharp twinge of justice but it was Verdandi who spoke out. "This warm skin provided by the esteemed and noble Chief is a gift, and has served us well."

"Forgive me if I offended you," chirped Hazel. "I am only curious as to what it is warming." She approached the table and lifted the skin. Verdandi swatted her hand away.

"Verdandi!" said Tess in surprise.

"We do not know this woman," said the apprentice, not taking her blue eyes from Hazel's green ones.

"I do know her. She is trustworthy. I can vouch for her." Tess's heart was pounding with the implications of her promise. But hadn't Hazel promised her the same bond of friendship?

"There, there, child," cooed Hazel, "I have just a touch of feminine curiosity. Surely you can relate to that."

"I suppose I can," relented Verdandi, but she staid her ground next to the table.

"Can I take a peek? There's a fresh apple pie in it for you if you say yes." Hazel winked at Tess and removed the lid from the basket she was carrying, revealing a round brown pie oozing with the scent of baked apples in the autumn air.

"Mmmm." Verdandi closed her eyes, inhaling the sweet smell.

"Go ahead," said Tess, "let her see. What harm will it do?"

Verdandi opened her eyes again and looked at the pie, then the table, then the pie again. "All right then," she said, and she slowly lifted the coyote skin from the table.

The witch admired the handiwork. She slid her fingers upon smooth wooden rods. She would discover the meaning behind this contraption; her curiosity and desire must be satisfied. "What magic is this?"

"This is no magic," said Verdandi. "This is technology."

"I see," said Hazel, lifting her eyebrows. "And what is its purpose?

"I am afraid I cannot relinquish that information yet," said Tess, joining them at the table. "But I can show you how it works."

Silk socks spun the fan-belt. An egg held itself in the radiator. Sawdust was tamped down in the gearbox to muffle any sound. Verdandi wound the pedals, and the machine whirred, thrusting a wind all around it.

"There is just one problem," said Tess. "One missing piece to the puzzle that I am trying to figure out." Tess and Verdandi and

T3 had managed to propel the machine across the flat ground, but had not achieved liftoff.

"Nothing a little apple pie won't fix," smiled Hazel.

Together, the three women sat on a blanket outside in the sun and shared the pie, making sure to save a piece for T3. "She'd never forgive us if we left her out of this," said Tess.

"Leave her out, apple pie, that's it!" exclaimed Verdandi. She turned to Hazel. You wouldn't happen to have a whole apple with you, would you?"

Hazel reached into her brown skirts. "Why yes, I do! You must be growing, girl, to still be hungry."

"Not to eat," said Verdandi, accepting the apple. "For the radial pump!" She dashed back inside and shoved the apple into a space between the gear shifter and the pedals. "Now try it," she said to Tess, who, with Hazel, had followed her in.

Tess rotated the pedals. Slowly at first, then building up steam. Within seconds, the spinning wheel lifted up from the table of its own accord.

"It is magic," breathed Hazel. The professor and apprentice paled and turned to her.

"You must keep this a secret. Please promise."

Hazel looked back and forth at the two strange women then settled her eyes upon the contraption. "I will keep your secret. What a brilliant young lady you are, Verdandi. What a brain you have to figure out how to achieve such an incredible feat against nature. What a wonder you are."

"No," said Verdandi shyly, "it is all the professor. She is the one responsible for this genius work. I simply added an apple. And thank you for that."

Tess burned with jealousy. She appreciated her student's praise, but it should have been directed at her from the beginning.

Now Hazel thought Verdandi was the smarter one. To be upstaged was one thing, but to be upstaged in front of a lover was quite another. Tess took three short breaths in an effort to reduce the tightness in her chest.

"This has been an interesting and exciting afternoon," said Hazel. "What say you and I take a walk in the woods to clear our heads in the cool air?"

"It is warm in here," admitted Tess. "Shall you be joining us?" she asked Verdandi.

The younger woman appraised her and Hazel. "No, I will continue my work here. If you could retrieve a pitcher of water on your way back, that would be exceedingly helpful." She handed two large leather flasks to the women as they stepped back into the sun.

CHAPTER 7

Hazel and Tess lay in a pile of dry crisp leaves and looked up at the sky.

"I've heard of a romp in the hay, but a romp in the leaves is even better," giggled Tess.

Hazel adjusted her arm beneath Tess's head. "This is the best time of year, and I am so glad I am able to spend it with you, amidst the glory of nature."

"I have never seen anything so beautiful," said Tess.

Hazel rolled over and looked at Tess deeply in the eyes. "Neither have I." She kissed her with a long persistence.

"I was worried you might not be impressed with me anymore, after seeing how talented Verdandi is."

Hazel licked her throat and whispered in her ear. "I only have eyes for you."

The leaves started crunching, with no wind.

Verdandi and T3 finished digging the thin trench around their hut. Just in time for a band of Puritans to come yomping from town through the woods.

"There is a witch!" came a voice from the throng. "Her red hair gives her away!"

Verdandi lingered in the doorway. A rock was thrown. Verdandi turned the newly fashioned knob of the door and enacted the defensive weaponry she and T3 had been working on all morning. A series of shields on wheels rolled from the back of the shack to the front, enclosing the little house. The rock bounced off. More rocks were thrown but they could not permeate the strong polished oak.

"Burn it down!" called a woman from the crowd. One man stepped forward and attempted to light the shields with his flint but they would not catch. "It is more witchcraft," he concluded. "We must address the reverend with this finding."

They marched back to town, new accusations forming in their collective minds.

A cold wind blew the leaves from the cuddled couple. The evening's first stars began to peek out alongside a round white moon. A raven cawed. Hazel smiled, her teeth reflecting the light of the night.

CHAPTER 8

The full moon shone like the sun on All Hallow's Eve. Hazel's eyes reflected the valiant light. Tonight, she would avenge her sisters. She would procure the elements needed for her survival. She would not be the next victim of the Salem Inquisition.

She had found the perfect scapegoat. Now for the perfect spell.

Hazel entered the foggy cemetery. The rusty gates screeched, thirsty for oil. Fresh plots were barely covered by pebbles, and the witch dug.

The raven circled around her before perching on her shoulder. "Yes, my special one, you will be instrumental in the secret scheme we devise to protect ourselves. If we don't, no one else will. We are in this for ourselves, for our own survival. And glory."

The wind blew the scarf from her face and her teeth glinted like a hungry wolf's fangs. She howled in delight. "Freedom and power, that is what we will gain tonight. If we plan well, the townsfolk will be shaking in their boots and worshipping me as the saviour of their pathetic community, and the reverend will be kissing my feet. Most importantly, those three women, and their nasty savage accomplices, will take the punishment doled out to me, and I will be rid of nosy intruders forever. The world around us will be mine." The bird screeched. "Yes, my confidante, my dear familiar, it will be yours, too."

In the shadow of the gallows, Hazel upturned the rocky soil beneath tombstones etched with skulls and angels blowing wasted souls into the ether. She traced her fingers upon the intricate designs, and hummed to herself.

"Double, triple, red headed trouble

Fires burn upon the rubble

No more in darkness will I shy

For tomorrow intruders are sure to fry"

She unearthed the remains of a recently deceased child. The cadaver was stiff and thin skin clung to brittle bones. "Beautiful," said Hazel, through gritted teeth. She pulled the skin from the face. "This is just what I need for my next sweet treat."

She then pried off the last flecks of flesh from the abandoned face and placed them in a mattrass tied to her apron. From her pockets she procured a thin pine stick. With a flick of her fingers, the end burned red. She spat into the jar and then stirred the contents with the long scrap of wood. The fatty flesh dissolved in her saliva. "Now the ingredients are prepared for the perfect concoction that will be irresistible to any young gal."

Closing the bolt head and returning the wand to her pocket, she cackled in glee. She left the crowded graveyard and continued to her own humble home on the far side of Blackbird Lake. Time to cook.

CHAPTER 9

By the time Hazel arrived at the scientists' cozy cottage, Tess and T3 had gone out to harvest food from the wild as Hazel had taught them to. T3 carried extra baskets supplied to them by the helpful Algonquin tribe.

Verdandi stayed in the small wigwam that cloistered the three of them. It was warm as she maneuvered discs and rearranged gears to combine into a way back home, when the moment would come. The salty wind outside blew against the enclosure to no avail. Verdandi and the homestead stayed put.

There was a knock at the door, first like an acorn, then a pebble, then a rock. Verdandi answered.

"Oh, it is you."

"Yes, it is I," said Hazel. "And I come bearing a gift. Let us not be against each other but for the common cause."

Verdandi's conscience twinged. She looked at the bright bauble held by the stem between Hazel's long fingers.

"What exactly is that? A glass fruit?"

"No, my dear; it is a candied apple, that I made just for you.

Verdandi considered her upside down reflection in the shiny apple. "It is as red as blood."

"As red as your hair," corrected the witch. "Go ahead, take it, eat it." She placed the glistening fruit into Verdandi's hands.

Verdandi felt the smooth orb and rolled it between her palms. In her prosthetic fingers, it felt cold and hard. To her flesh fingers, it felt smooth. She was curious.

"Taste it, just give it a bite," Hazel coaxed.

Verdandi hesitated.

"I imagine it has been a while since you have indulged in such sweetness. You are a grown woman, but there is no shame in retaining a child's desires."

It was true; with the brilliant yet picky Tess as her mentor, there had not been many visceral treats in her life the past few years. Verdandi did not realize how much she missed the joy of candy until now. Yet, something stopped her.

"Thank you for the gift. Perhaps I shall wait until Tess and T3 return and we can all four share it together."

Hazel's eyes narrowed. "You are refusing my kindness?" She softened her voice. "I meant this to be enjoyed by you, my dear. You deserve it. I see all the tribulation you have been through as of late, and I think your hard work should be rewarded."

Verdandi thought about her recent tinkering. "Yes, I have been working hard, but Tess says that hard work is its own reward."

"Indeed, she would say something like that," smiled Hazel. "Yet there is no sin in partaking of a gift. In fact, to ignore my offering would risk insult."

"I am sorry," said Verdandi. "I would not mean to offend you." The red ripe glistening apple was tempting. She swallowed her saliva.

"Take just one bite," Hazel said eagerly, leaning forward with her hands pressed together as if in prayer. "Taste and see the goodness of the Lord."

Verdandi lifted the apple to her lips. It shone in the midday autumn sun, like a new planet yet to be discovered. The wind swirled a whirlwind of leaves about her. She bit, her strong white teeth cracking through the hard candied shell to the sweet fruit beneath. She moaned.

"This is delicious."

"Indeed, that is the name of the apple I chose for you. The ruby sheen reflects your flaming red hair wonderfully, like a growing fire."

Verdandi took another bite, tasting the sweet and sour flavours mingle in her mouth as her teeth chomped shards of bone hard candy and soft flesh together. She had never experienced a food like this. She opened her mouth for a third bite and yawned.

"Feeling sleepy, my dear?" asked Hazel. She guided the young woman to the bumpy bed in the bungalow. Leaves flew in with them and scattered over Verdandi as she lay sprawled out. Her eyes closed.

"Sleep, girl, never to awaken again." Hazel's green eyes glowed in the semidarkness. She grinned with a smile that stretched from ear to ear. Covering her mouth with her scarf, she left for her next mission. The reverend would be waiting for her.

CHAPTER 10

The Algonquin medicine woman appeared at the door where Tess was crying as she held Verdandi's hands. T3 was stroking the cold forehead of the unmoving girl. She lay upon the leafy mattress like a statue; an angel guarding souls in a cemetery.

The medicine woman used a small wooden bowl to wet Verdandi's lips with a syrupy liquid that smelled strongly of alcohol. Then she unhooked the girl's corset and rubbed a thick milky ointment on her chest and throat.

Verdandi woke up retching. Blood and mucous covered her and the bed. The smell of decaying flesh filled the air. Together, Tess and T3 carried the weakened young woman to the river where they dunked her in the chilly current, causing goosebumps to cover her entire naked body. Her hair was rinsed of vomit, creating a pool of redness that looked like a halo of blood around her head. Finally, they pulled her from the water, wrapped her in a wide colourful cloth supplied by the Algonquin tribe, and then covered her in the coyote skin.

Tess held the young woman in her arms, rocking the swaddled figure like a baby. To think she had been jealous of this beautiful creature, her apprentice, who she now realized was like a daughter to her.

"Outshine me little star, for someday you will be the sun and I will be a remembrance of light."

Verdandi's eyes fluttered open. Her hazy gaze filled Tess's heart with joy.

"I love you, dear child, I am so sorry for ever mistreating you in any way, please come back to me and I will share in our inventions together. Just please, don't die." Her voice cracked at the last words and she began crying again.

T3 knelt down and wrapped her arms around them. "She's going to be okay. Chief will make sure of that." She turned her head and looked up at the powerful and kind leader, and then shifted her eyes to the medicine woman. "Thank you both, thank you all, for saving us once again."

"That is what the human family is for," answered Chief. She placed a hand upon T3's head. T3 rose and they embraced.

"Listen, she is saying something," exclaimed Tess. "What is it Verdandi, who did this to you?"

"Hazel... witch. Witch... Hazel," she murmured.

"We need witch hazel for your antidote?" asked Tess. She called out to T3. "We need witch hazel! Quick, forage in the forest; I know you will come across some if you look!"

Chief released her comforting hold on T3. "Pause and reflect," she said. "It sounds as if there is a different meaning to her message."

Verdandi persisted in her weak words. "Witch, Hazel."

T3 looked at Chief incredulously. "Are you trying to say that Verdandi is telling us that Hazel Feathergill is a witch?"

Chief nodded her head sadly.

"Tsk! There is no such person as a witch," retorted Tess.

The medicine woman stepped forward to look directly into her eyes. "Indeed, there are such creatures as witches. Not the sort of innocents whom the Puritans seek, but rather, wicked hearts beating in human bodies, intent on enchantments and miserable power that can only be brought about by magic. My antidote to the witch's poison was blessed by our ancestors and enhanced with their loving powers of health. The concoction used by this witch you know was connived from the depths of death, without eternal life, but explicit damnation."

Verdandi sat up, still shivering even as her red crown shone in the waning sunset. "It is true, I would not have believed it, but I am convinced. You can call it science, you can call it chemistry, but it boils down to witchcraft. Maybe not magic, but indeed deadly in force and meant for harm, not enhancement." She looked up at Tess whose eyes still wept in relief. "I know you do not want to believe it, but Hazel's actions bear her true intent. You and I have always worked for progress, for the common good. Hazel's intent is for her own provisions, her own desires, her own dark motives. Beware, dear professor, lest you be next to succumb to her wiles. As indeed it seems you already have."

"Love can be an enchantment of sorts," Tess pondered. She wiped her eyes. "Never ever think for a moment that my love for you isn't true. I do love you, dear child, and I do not know how I could attain success or feel fulfilled without you. I promise from here on to take care of you, not just as my apprentice, but as my daughter. You are precious to me. I trust you. If you say beware, I will cast aside my rosy haze and see with fresh discernment that which you call evil. I believe you."

"There is only one way to find out for sure," piped in T3.

"Surely you don't mean by drowning her?" gasped Tess.

"No, I don't adhere to that hogwash. I mean by conducting a reconnaissance mission."

Verdandi lifted herself up to her feet and turned to the medicine woman. "Thank you for the analeptic. I believe your antidote has not just saved me, but also strengthened me. I feel refreshed, as if I have just awoken from a deep sleep. Let me put some food in my empty stomach, and we can discuss our next steps."

Tess and Verdandi walked back to their little hut. T3 lingered behind, and held the Chief's hand. Then she looked up into her broad beautiful brown eyes.

"When it comes my time, don't let them hang me like a dog; rather shoot me like a soldier."

"Your time will come on its own accord," answered Chief. She kissed T3's forehead. "No harm will come to you on my watch."

T3 glowed in the warmth of faith.

CHAPTER 11

The trio grew weary. They were tired out from collecting items for the flying machine. It would be the perfect vehicle to spy on the small Puritan town without being seen. Metal was unfound, so they searched for the strongest fallen branches with which to create their invention. They still needed to figure out conductivity and hopefully a way to transmit energy and transport matter without blowing themselves to smithereens.

Finally, with their combined talents, Tess, Verdandi, and T3 prepared the engine for its first flight. They had modified an Algonquin canoe, adding propellers and a gear shaft, to create a quiet and quick flying machine. Tess boarded the open cockpit with Verdandi nestled in close behind her. They wrapped scarves around their faces to keep them warm from the jetting wind. T3 cranked the engine, and with a whoosh, they were off.

"What a brilliant idea you had, to spy on Salem from above without being detected."

"Not many people think to look up," said the apprentice humbly.

"We have a real birds-eye view from here," said Tess. She moaned.

"What is it?"

"I am missing Lamarr."

"Which one?"

"All of them."

Verdandi pulled the gear shift towards her and reached forward to pat Tess on her left shoulder. "I do too." They soared higher with the wind pushing their thin woven sails.

Below them they could see Gallow's Hill, the cemetery, the house with seven gables, and a small village. People swarmed between the buildings in the town square as fear mongers stepped upon boxes. Tess and Verdandi could hear them shouting cries of witchcraft and rebellion, evil and justice. Cheering crowds drew closer.

"That doesn't look good," said Tess over the flapping sound of propellers.

"Neither does that," said Verdandi. "Look starboard!"

Tess peered down to her right. Her scarf came undone and floated slowly to the ground. "What am I looking at?"

Tess squinted her eyes in the wind. Verdandi's younger eyes were sharper.

"It is Hazel, entering the church as a man of the cloth holds the door open."

"Not good," said Tess.

"Wildly suspicious," agreed Verdandi. They turned the flying machine back to their little home base.

CHAPTER 12

Hazel watched a red scarf fall from the sky. She bent over to pick it up.

The minister breathed heavily through a thick black cloth strapped behind his ears. Hazel wore a white mask over her head, emulating a giant raven's skull.

"Greetings, Goodwoman Hazel Feathergill."

"And greetings to you, Reverend Jeremiah Thorndale."

Together they entered the church. It was dark with only one window allowing light to struggle through bracken windows. Candlelight wavered with the opening and closing of the heavy door. The two figures shifted in the dimness and sat upon straight backed wooden pews.

Reverend Thorndale spoke first. "I am willing to believe your innocence, if you can prove the guilt of those demon women living amongst the savages. Otherwise, I will make sure you burn, lighting a match to the pyre myself."

Goodwoman Feathergill felt her skin prickle. Fury at his audaciousness fueled her words. "There will be no fire for me but for the blaze of this church if threats against me come to reality."

The reverend opened his ever present Bible and flipped through dogeared pages of underlined passages. "But I suffer not a woman to teach, nor to usurp authority over the man, but to be in silence. For Adam was first formed, then Eve. And Adam was not deceived, but the woman being deceived was in the transgression. Notwithstanding she shall be saved in childbearing, if they continue in faith and charity and holiness with sobriety."

The reflection of the cross from the altar upon the reverend's glasses made Hazel feel dizzy. She refocused on his words.

"Are you a foot washer or a stone thrower, Reverend?"

"Of course I always have the greater good for God as my main mission," he huffed.

"With that in mind as our first prerogative, we must cleanse this scourge upon our town. The only way to follow your holy vows and attain a peaceful village is to cast out the doom hovering along the perimeter."

"You mean the savages, of course," answered the man.

"That goes without saying. Yet there is a more powerful threat to our village, one that could tear it and us apart. Ripping like skin from flesh. These entities must be blackened in the pyre of the church's faith. The townspeople cry out for blood, the grease of witches. I can deliver that to you. I can reveal the monsters that live on the boundary of our beautiful and steadfast home.

"How do you intend to do that?"

"There are the three women who survive on the threshold of the savage devils.   Two are just alike, exactly in form and manner; only witchcraft could produce such an anomaly. The third is their servant, bearing the red hair of demonic flames. Her right hand and arm are not human. They are a monstrous combination of strange material like gleaming bone and whipped leather. Her very being is an abomination to your holy church, and to the town of Salem which you have sworn to protect and govern as a man of faith. You have no choice but to persecute these wily females before they further bewitch your flock. Their presence is disastrous."

"So, you will reveal these women in exchange for what?"

"My innocence." Her whisper echoed through her long beaked mask. "They must die for it. Or else great peril will come to you personally. I guarantee it."

A sudden draft extinguished the struggling candles. "Do we have a deal?"

The reverend shivered. "Yes, Goodwoman, we do."

CHAPTER 13

The Puritans arrived at the little home by the rising of the moon. The bright orb and dazzling stars competed against the torches burning below, in a mobbed constellation. The townsfolk carried their lights and their weapons; pitchforks and shovels, smoothbore muskets and snaphaunces. Hazel Feathergill and Reverend Thorndale led the clamourous crowd.

"How could you betray me? I thought you loved me!" Tess stood in the doorway with tears streaming down her cheeks like a rainy moon. T3 pulled her inside and Verdandi enacted the shield, but to Tess, the danger was overshadowed by heartbreak.

The reverend couldn't believe his eyes upon glimpsing Tess and her clone. "They have returned from the dead!"

Tess was devoid of all pride as she clung to T3. "I am sorry for treating you poorly, as a non-human. I am ashamed at my previous notions."

"All is forgiven," said T3. "Now it is time to fight." Just then a pitchfork jabbed Tess in the ribs and she yelled out in pain. It jammed the shield so that it could not close all the way. Verdandi and T3 tried pulling and pushing it along its track, but the rake budged too late.

"It's thaumaturgy!" shouted a voice from the horde.

"Nay, it is metalurgy," said another.

"NO, cried out the loudest. It is witchcraft! Grab the witches, and we will hang them on Gallows Hill!"

Tess and T3 were grabbed. Verdandi shimmied up to the roof and hopped off. She uncovered the blanket of leaves that had been hiding the airship, and breezed off across the woods towards the river. "Birds need their flock," she thought, and she flew like a whisper in the blinking sky.

CHAPTER 14

Tess and T3 were marched and pulled and shoved to Gallow's Hill where two nooses already awaited them. Just as the wound rope touched Tess's neck, there was a blast of wind and a flurry of leaves. Verdandi held tight to the professor as she flew by, rescuing her from a hanging death.

The crowd gasped and screamed. "Quick, kill the other witch!" came the cry.

"Kill the witch, kill the witch," the Puritans chanted. T3 felt open air meet her dangling feet. This was it, she thought, her time had come.

Then an arrow sliced the air, and with it the knot that held T3's neck. She dropped to the leafy ground with an ungraceful thud. Suddenly, a pair of strong, weather-worn hands snatched her up and untied the tangled knot, releasing her from certain death.

T3 looked into the eyes of her saviour. "Chief!" she exclaimed in a hoarse voice.

Chief handed her a bow and a quiver of arrows. "No time to talk now. Remember what we have practiced." She kissed the clone's mouth and for a millisecond, all the chaos faded away.

"I'll remember," whispered T3, and she aimed her first arrow.

Tess gratefully accepted the tribe's fervent help without question. She was not an army of one anymore, trying to prove herself to the world. Now she was part of a community trying to save what was good and defeat what was evil. She adjusted herself into the cockpit and lowered the sails.

"Ready?" she shouted back to Verdandi.

"Always!"

A fierce cackle trickled through the wind. It was Hazel, pointing her wooden wand at them. "Don't climb higher than you can fly, little birds!" A bullet of flame shot from her wand, followed by another, and another, until the long airship was full of holes and descended with a rolling crash.

CHAPTER 15

Tess and Verdandi scrambled from their wrecked airship. "Here, grab these," said Verdandi, throwing her two balls.

"Rocks?"

"No," said the teen, lighting the flint. "Bombs."

Tess tripped over a discarded broomstick. Verdandi threw the first noxious bomb towards the Puritans. As the wick burned, it released a poisonous odour not unlike a skunk's spray. The Puritans began coughing and wheezing.

Tess hastily converted some of the less mangled parts of the airship's engine to fit the broom. She pedaled the whirring wheel with her hands and there was lift off! The direction was guided by leaning to and fro, and side to side.

"Yippee!" she cried out, first in delight that her ingenuity had worked. Then she called out again, "For my sisters!" and she dove at the reverend with her bomb. His hacking cough was her reward. "Toss me some more, Verdandi!"

The apprentice removed bombs from her deep apron pockets and lit them one by one before throwing them to the hovering Tess. Then Tess flew high above, crossing the moon with her deep silhouette, before dropping the poison gas onto her targets. The night sky filled with smoggy fumes.

The gaseous cloud was joined by a green mist floating from the cemetery. With the mist came an army of such despicable horror that Tess almost fell off her broom upon witnessing it. Reverend Thorndale screamed in terror at the supernatural sight. Hazel laughed and spun her wand like a baton between her lithe fingers.

"Come all zombies, ghouls, and ghosts

Bring your powers of the most

bewitched bedraggled beguiling sort

and we will end this, starboard to port."

Her wand burned red on both ends as she conjured spirits of the dead, unsaved souls, and walking corpses from their resting places. With shrieks of anger and agonizing death, they paraded past the Puritans and encircled the three time travelers. Tess's broom sputtered and sank with the condensation filling her fuel pump. They were doomed.

"What have you done?" cried Reverend Thorndale. Hazel turned to him slowly, still spinning her wand. Her green eyes glowed eerily in the growing darkness. "I have ensured my fortune. If you have thoughts of rearing your unholy head against me, I have my army of the undead to protect me and see me through."

The reverend fell to his knees and began praying. Hazel kicked the Bible from his clutches and sent it soaring into the moonlight, where it was trampled beneath skeletal feet. "Only I can save you now," she hissed.

The deadly undead could not be defeated. They had no life to lose, and so, they reached their bony fingers out, scratching flesh from T3's shoulder. A purple light flashed by her eyes, and the yellow skeleton exploded into two hundred pieces. T3 scurried up and adjusted her arrow in the bow. Chief stood next to her and raised her fishing spear. Their eyes met in psychic understanding. They raised their weapons and led the charge together.

The Algonquin elders called upon their spiritual ancestors to fight with them and for them. Each arrowhead, each sharpened axe, each heavy club glowed purple with their blessed touch. The mystical battle raged on with supernatural powers proving stronger than conventional weaponry.

Still, the undead kept coming; willowy ghosts and ghastly goblins appeared, gnashing their jagged teeth.

"You will burn for this, witch!" shouted Reverend Thorndale to Hazel.

Her shriek rose above the sounds of melee. "Not before you suffer for your disbelief! You should have trusted me to lead all along. Now you turn your back on me? So shall you die." A trio of goblins attacked the huddled man and tore the flesh from his bony back, then his throat, then his face. They ate ravenously, blood dripping down their pointed grey chins.

A bloodcurdling scream repeated itself in short bursts across the sky as a dark shadow loomed over the battle. Chief pointed above T3's head, and she nodded. She let her arrow fly. With a final squawk, Hazel's beloved raven fell unceremoniously to the ground.

"My familiar!" shouted the witch. She felt her power ebb as the lights in her wand diffused to blackness.

The ground rumbled. Four horsemen dressed in black aligned their beasts across the wicked trail where Hazel stood screaming. They encircled her, closing in closer and closer.

"You will never get me, you weaklings! Never!" Her wand glowed again with a furious red flame.

Then the earth shook again. It made a sound of falling trees. The sand beneath the horses hooves began to sift away, downward, into a thin crack in the earth. The crack grew longer and wider. The riders hastily retreated before they were sucked into a sinkhole.

Again, the ground trembled, and with a bolt of lightening, it tore open, creating a jagged hole like a broken zipper. Hazel slid down into the sand now pouring down, down, into nothingness. She tried to grab at rocks, at tree roots, at anything, to keep above ground. In her confusion, she dropped her stick.

"No! Not my wand," she wailed.

Tess swung the rope that had been tied around T3's neck. Like a lasso, she threw it towards Hazel. "Grab on!"

"I don't need your tyrannical mercy! I will die before succumbing to the likes of you!"

"And so you will," said T3, watching as the earth parted wider, swallowing the witch up without fail. She disappeared into the crevice.

"I'm falling, I'm falling! Curse you all!" Hazel shouted until there was a flash of green lightening and a billow of putrid smoke rising from the charred earth.

The army of the dead dissipated, soaring with howls into the night.

The Puritans fell to the ground and cried out to the Native people encircling them. "Please do not kill us! Let us bury our fallen brethren in a godly manner before you slaughter us, at least! Have mercy, have mercy," they pleaded.

Chief stepped into the middle of the sweating, crying, urinating throng. "We will show you the mercy you would not perceive possible for us. We will do it your way, through court."

"No, do not judge us!" cried a man with wet pants.

"You will judge yourselves." Chief turned back to her tribe. "Tie them up and deliver them to their place of worship. They can be tried for their crimes there." She walked over to T3 and kissed dirt from her face before addressing the survivors again. "When you are done, we will retire by a grande campfire. All who pledge allegiance are welcome."

CHAPTER 16

In the small church the next morning, the captured Puritans, the few who had survived, sat tied together by their wrists and ankles in a row along a hard straight backed pew. On the jury were six Algonquin Natives, and six Puritans who had surrendered. Chief held court, standing grandely behind the massive lectern.

T3 and Verdandi stood by the door of the musty, echoing building. Despite the autumn sun shining through the sparse dirty windows, Tess felt cold in her joints as she sat upon the witness stand, which had been the reverend's throne-like chair.

In her clear teaching voice, the professor testified. "Magic is a technology that we do not yet understand. I have witnessed phenomenon that I can explain, and others that require more research. The ability to perform such modern day miracles is not witchcraft, but science. Things my own eyes cannot decipher as being real can be trusted to further study. Everything on this earth has a rational explanation, even though we do not always know what that is. Those of us who partake in the study of such magic are not witches, but scientists. With knowledge gleaned from study, from experiments, from the wisdom of others, we can form calculated opinions based on truth, not hearsay."

"Are you stating that these townspeople, who accused you of witchcraft, each of them individually or collectively, are then innocent?"

"I would say that they are ignorant, yet not innocent. Not knowing and judging without facts is unjust. However, their gossip went past being unjust to being criminal. Lives were lost. That could have been avoided. Justice could have prevailed against what evil entered Salem, without bloodshed. So in my opinion, each and all of these people are guilty."

The accused Puritans wept in shame and fear, and some clenched their fists in outrage.

The jury withdrew to the tabernacle to discuss the fates of the accused.

"We find the defendants guilty on all charges. Their punishment is banishment. Never again may these people return to Salem, although they are free to join other settlements as they may find suitable.

"Let it be so,"said Chief. And so it was.

CHAPTER 17

"Now what?" asked Verdandi.

"Time to head home." Tess hugged the girl close to her. "I am so very proud of you. You should be proud of yourself, too.

"I am," admitted the apprentice with a flush.

Together they stood beneath the portal they had rigged up. Tess held Verdandi's hand. "Because of your future technology we will be able to travel back in time, to the present."

Chief shook her head. "I still do not understand the mechanisms you have configured."

"Not to worry," said T3. "I can teach you all about it."

"Wait," Tess frowned. "Are you not coming back with us?"

"I am choosing not to, dear sister, but I appreciate everything you have done for me. I feel like I am equally needed, and wanted here." She cast a shy smile to Chief.

"You are," Chief grinned.

"You could still use this time machine to visit us, or stay with us, any time you want," offered Verdandi.

"Of course," said T3, giving Tess and Verdandi one last hug. "I will see you again, back in the future. Or you may return here."

"This invention is going to open up new and exciting opportunities for justice throughout the ages, for all people," said Tess.

"I am sure it will," said T3. "Starting with us."

Tess squeezed Verdandi's hand tighter. "Are you ready?"

"Always," said the young woman.

"All right then, flip the switch!"

Tess and Chief pulled the pair of horseshoes down to set free the current that would blast the professor and apprentice back to their own time. Or fry them.

The earth shook and green lightening shot from beyond the sky.

CHAPTER 18

Tess and Verdandi stepped into the laboratory in amazement. They ran outside to see if they were, indeed, truly home.

What they saw did not assure them.

The present has changed subtly. The buildings were more like warm wigwams instead of chilly boxed houses, and the air was cleansed of coal dust, clear to see for miles, as windmills provided hydropower. It was a quiet yet still bustling landscape without the roar of heavy engines.

Together they walked to the centre of town. "My gracious," said Tess, pointing at a large bronze sculpture." "It is I!"

Verdandi looked closer. I think you are mistaken. Read the plaque."

"Upon the commemoration of this day, 4 July 1694, the Algonquin town of Alset has been set in stone."

"Breathtaking," whispered Tess.

"I always thought so," came a deep voice behind her. The smell of leather and whale oil permeated the air. She knew who it was without having to look.

"Hugh." She turned around.

Their eyes met. "Can you ever forgive me?" she asked tearfully.

"One squabble will not make or break us," said the mechanic. He took her warmly in his arms.

"I won't let pride get in my way again."

"Nor will I let you."

The reconciled couple kissed with urgent passion.

"Hey, you two, look at this!"

Tess and Hugh dislodged tongues but still held onto each other. Verdandi pressed a button and opened a large blue closet standing in the middle of the square. She pulled out an object that had been hanging within. The sign above the closet read in yellow letters, "Free Public Transportation."

"My gracious, the present is more than I realized it could be."

Hugh looked at her quizzically. "I will explain it all to you soon. Just know, change can be a good thing."

Hugh grinned. "There seems to be a change in you, and I certainly like it."

Verdandi mounted the broom and valiantly flew over the new and improved city.

Acknowledgements

Thank you to my Kickstarter heroes who funded this beautiful book cover by Steven Novak Illustrations:

Ashley Grant, Captin Jim Pekoe, Douglas Yeager, Quentin Stockwell, Heidi Welch, Rita McAuliffe, Elizabeth Chatsworth, and Cathy.

Also in appreciation to the host of The Writers Circus, author R.D. Trimble, for his continual support of authors.

With high regard for the curators at the Peabody Essex Museum and the Salem tour guides who fulfilled my quest for facts in my fiction.

Exceptional thanks to my BETA readers.

Gratitude goes to my devoted editor.

Great thanks to the talented musician and storyteller John Joe Baxter who never failed to entertain me during my daily writing breaks.

Also by Jessica Lucci

The Watch City Trilogy:

Waltham Watch

Subton Switch

Gustover Glitch

Short story collections:

Steampunk Leap Year

Steampunk New Year

Tequila Sheila and Other Tall Tales

Steampunk Pride

Middle grade fiction:

Weird

Children's Fiction:

Lunch Time Choo-Choo

Poetry:

Poetry in the Prose of Watch City: Waltham Watch

Poetry Pouring (from Subton Switch)

Poems Fly (from Gustover Glitch)

Love Watch City

Coming Soon by Jessica Lucci

The Snow Globe and Other Holiday Stories

Seven holiday stories are filled with the whimsy of different genres including paranormal, romance, science fiction, fantasy, and yes, steampunk!

About the Author

Jessica Lucci is a multi genre author of more than twenty books including the IHIBRP 5 Star Award winner "Justice for the Lemon Trees" and the 2019 Lesfic Bard Book Awards Finalist, "Subton Switch." Throughout her books run themes of freedom and inclusivity. She makes her home in New England where she is currently writing a steampunk romance.

Website: www.jessicalucci.org

Amazon:
https://www.amazon.com/Jessica-Lucci/e/B075JMNK1S%3Fref=dbs_a_mng_r wt_scns_share

Etsy:
https://www.etsy.com/shop/JessicaLucciBooks?ref=seller-platform-mcnav

Please leave a review on Amazon! It helps me, and I love seeing my reader's thoughts.

Your Page

This is your page, dear Reader, to write in as you wish.

Made in the USA
Middletown, DE
02 October 2021